THE
UXBRIDGE
ENGLISH
DICTIONARY

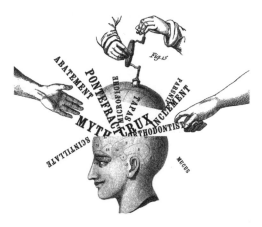

Fig. 15

ABATEMENT
PONTEFRACT
MICROFIBRE
TAPAS
PASSIONFRUIT
MYTP
CRUX
ORTHODONTIST
INCLEMENT
SCINTILLATE
MUCUS

THE UXBRIDGE

UNIVERSITY
PRESS

The UXBRIDGE ENGLISH DICTIONARY is indebted to
Bill Bailey, Jack Dee, Stephen Fry, Andy Hamilton,
Jeremy Hardy, Tony Hawks, Harry Hill,
Ross Noble, Linda Smith and Sandi Toksvig
for their outstanding contributions,
and to the many listeners to
'I'M SORRY I HAVEN'T A CLUE' who urged us
to publish this book in the first place.

HarperCollinsEntertainment
An Imprint of HarperCollinsPublishers
77–85 Fulham Palace Road, Hammersmith, London W6 8JB
www.harpercollins.co.uk

Published by HarperCollinsEntertainment 2005
1 3 5 7 9 8 6 4 2

Copyright © Tim Brooke-Taylor, Barry Cryer, Graeme Garden, Jon Naismith & Iain Pattinson
The Authors assert the moral right to be identified as the authors of this work
A catalogue record for this book is available from the British Library
ISBN 0 00 720337 3
Set in Consort and American Typewriter
Illustrations by Tony McSweeney
Printed and bound in Great Britain by Clays Limited, St Ives Plc

THE UXBRIDGE ENGLISH DICTIONARY

SEVENTEENTH EDITION
(Approx.)

TIM BROOKE-TAYLOR
BARRY CRYER
GRAEME GARDEN
JON NAISMITH
IAIN PATTINSON

Introduction

Uxbridge University has always had a bad press. This has been of little concern to our graduates, many of whom have soon discovered that an Uxbridge education is something that gets you noticed. When they inform the Human Resources Appointment Enablement Selection Interview Board of any of the world's finest blue-chip multinationals that they have been to Uxbridge, they can rest assured that (so long as they're only slightly misheard) their application will go straight to the top of the pile.

Are you sometimes alarmed at the pace of life in our 21st Century? Today we have fast cars, fast food, fast women, zip fasteners and instant gratification. However there is a growing movement against this trend, and it's known simply as 'slow'. At The University of Uxbridge we are at the very forefront of 'slow' learning. In fact, our slow learners are some of the slowest around.

*The University
of Uxbridge*

Of course, the older a language gets the more complicated it becomes. Such are the many complexities of our English tongue that it can be very confusing trying to tell the subtle difference in meaning between similar words. For example, many people are entirely ignorant of the difference in correct usage between 'further' and 'farther'. Well, 'further' is used in the figurative rather than the physical sense to express 'a greater extent' or a 'progress towards a more advanced situation'. Whereas 'farther' is what your daddy is called when you grow up.

Here at the Uxbridge University Press, we don't pretend to be experts in the field of lexicography. We don't pretend to be any good at it at all. But what we do pretend is that this book, which has taken many editions and several contributors to get right, is one of the most worthwhile additions to any living room, library or lavatory you are likely to find, with or without a substantial price discount. If you abhor the fragrant misregard for basic English constriction, rest assured: this book will help you to keep your feet firmly on terra cotta.

THE EDITOR

N. V. Q. De Ploma
(DEAN, VICE-CHANCELLOR, P.E. TUTOR)

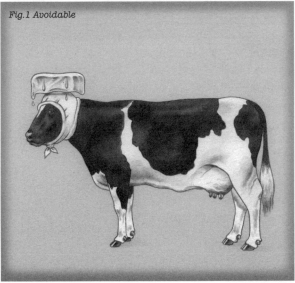

Fig.1 Avoidable

Aa

Aardvark
Harmless quadruped
cf. 'aardvark never killed anybody'

Abacus
Swedish swear word

Abatement
Downstairs storage area used by man with sinus trouble

Abattoir
Three-in-a-bed in a monastery

Abort
Sea-faring vessel from the Midlands

Acapulco
An unaccompanied Mexican

Accomplish
A drunken sidekick

Acolyte
Easy-listening clarinet music

Acupuncture
Very deliberate tyre slashing

Adder
Tasteless boast

Fig.2 Acupuncture

Alcoholic
Someone who drinks more than their doctor

Algebra
A brassière made out of kelp

Alimony
Backstreet currency

Alkaline
A queue at Alcoholics Anonymous

Aa

Alligator
Someone who accuses you of things

Almoner
An expensive meal

Angiogram
Irish folk singer

Announce
28 grams

Antelope
To run off with your
mother's sister

Fig.3 Aperitif

Antidisestablishmentarianism
Wife of strangely named Northern uncle

Aperitif
Cockney dentures

Apex
Gorilla's wristwatch

Arcane
Liverpudlian bamboo

Archery
Lying under oath and at all other times

Arizona
The person who 'Arry belongs to

Aromatic
A handy gadget used by
Robin Hood

Arsenic
Having sat on a razor blade

Artefact
Pretentious statistic

Fig.4 Arsenic

Aa

Artery
Shooting arrows at paintings

Aspire
The pointy bit on a church

Assassination
An arrangement to meet a donkey

Asymmetry
Place where you bury stiffs

Atrophy
Something you win at sport

Autobiography
A car service book

Autocue
Traffic jam

Avoidable
What a cow with a headache does

Fig.5 Atrophy

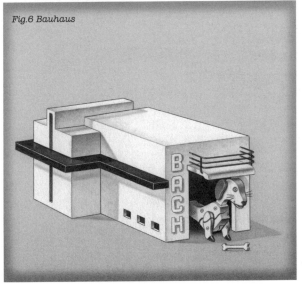

Fig.6 Bauhaus

Bb

Bacteria
Returning more upset than when you left

Balderdash
A rapidly receding hairline

Banquette
A tiny shag

Banshee
Gentlemen's club

Baptist
A junior hamburger chef

Barometric
Euro gardening aid

Barrel-organ
Brewer's droop

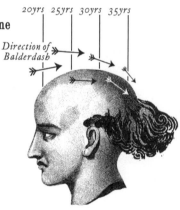

20yrs 25yrs 30yrs 35yrs

Direction of Balderdash

Fig. 7 Balderdash

Bacteria – Bigamist

Bathos
Unsuccessful musketeer

Bauhaus
Dog kennel

Beatitude
Stroppy mood common in teenage insects

Bedlam
A very favourite sheep

Bicycle
a. A double-headed corn-cutter;
b. An icicle that swings both ways

Bidet
Two days before D-Day

Bigamist
A larger than usual fog

Fig.8 Bicycle

Bb

Bigotry
A lumberjack's boast

Bile
An Australian bundle of hay

Biology
The science of why women shop

Biopsy
An organic gypsy

Biro
a. To purchase fish eggs;
b. Property developer

Bishopric
An unpopular member of the clergy

Blame
Walking with a blimp

Fig.9 Blame

Blandish
Michael Aspel

Boa constrictor
South African truss

Bollocks
Unsuccessful Botox

Bonsai
Dyslexic kamikaze pilot

Boulangerie
To heckle underwear

Boundary
Ungentlemanly
behaviour

Boutique
To heckle wood

Fig.10 Boutique

Bb

Bordello
Blasé greeting

Bratwürst
Macaulay Culkin

Brouhaha
Jolly tea party

Bustard
A very rude omnibus driver

Buttercup
Face down

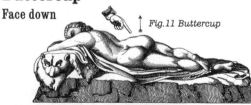

Fig.11 Buttercup

Buttress
A woman who keeps interrupting

Fig.12 Childhood

Cc

Cabaret
A wide range of available taxis

Cabbage
Nonsense spoken by taxi drivers

Caddy
Rather like a cad

Can-can
Tintin's partner

Candid
Past tense of 'can do'

Cannibalistic
A Geordie missile

Canoodle
To fondle in a small boat

Cantaloupe
Unable to run off and get married

Cantankerous
Chain of shops that sell tanks

Canteen
One who has reached the age of consent

Cantilever
The switch on an electric horse

Capsule
Better than Christmas

Carpentry
A 'way in' for
ornamental fish

Carping
To do a fish impression

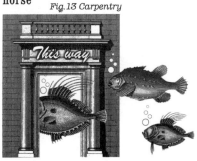

Fig. 13 Carpentry

Cc

Castigate
To have a nasty accident climbing into a field

Catalyst
A three-legged moggie

Cataract
Japanese for Cadillac

Cathartic
When the bag freezes

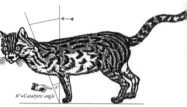

Fig.14 Catalyst

Caustic
A foul-mouthed parasite

Cenotaph
A Welsh laxative

Chairs
A toast by the Queen

Charabancs
The cleaning lady's a goer

Castigate – Circumspect

Chary
Rather like a chair

Childhood
A very young gangster

Chutzpah
A character in Shakespeare's
'Henry V'

Ciabatta
The Wookie in 'Star Wars'

Cinquecento
A hundred year old Chinaman

Circumnavigation
A Bar Mitzvah on a cruise liner

Fig.15 Cinquecento

Circumspect
a. The point of view of a Rabbi;
b. Spotted dick

Cc

Clarify
To domesticate the Grundys

Climate
The motto of The Everest Club

Co-opt
Brainwashed by a leading
supermarket chain

Cockaleekie
Prostate problem

Cocoa bean
An ex-clown

Codicil
Buffalo Bill's window box

Coffee
Someone who is coughed upon

Fig. 16 Cocoa bean

Clarify – Conclude

Coiffeur
A pretentious drinker

Coincidental
Having matching teeth

Collie-wobbles
A three-legged sheep dog

Colonnade
A fizzy enema

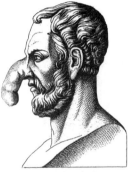

Fig. 17 Conclude

Comatose
Foot's gone dead

Combat
An aggressive marsupial

Conclude
An obscenely shaped nose

Cc

Condense
To fool the stupid

Condominium
A chemist's shop

Conurbation
What convicts do alone in their cells late at night

Context
A prison library book

Contraband
U.S. backed counter-
revolutionary orchestra

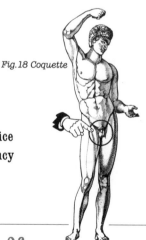
Fig. 18 Coquette

Copulate
The time it takes the police
to show up in an emergency

Coquette
Small penis

Corridor
Entrance to the Rover's Return

Counterpane
Someone who works in the Post Office

Countryside
To kill Piers Morgan

Crèche
A car accident in Woking

Crescendo
Termination of child care

Cross-country
Iraq

Crux
Middle class villains

Fig. 19 Cross-country

Cc

Crystallise
A retirement gift for Lord Nelson

Culotte
Post Office

Curate
A doctor

Custard
To swear after stepping in something

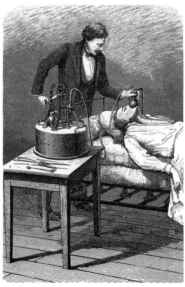

Fig.20 Curate

Dd

Fig.21 Domineering

Dd

Daiwoo
The host of 'Supermarket Sweep'

Damnation
Holland

Fig.22 Damnation

Dandelion
A big camp cat

Debasement
De room under de
ground floor

Decade
Ant

Decease
To stop stopping

Deft
Ebsolutely med

Deglaze
To stop watching 'Neighbours'

Delectable
Iain Duncan-Smith

Deliberate
To imprison

Delight
To make things go dark

Fig.23a Delight

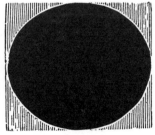

Fig.23b Delight

Dd

Demistifier
A retired magician

Derelict
A pleasant experience
in Ireland

Fig.24 Descant

Descant
A white collar insect

Deserted
The pudding's done a runner

Diamante
Way to start letter to 2nd World War Field Marshall

Diarrhoea
Ugly bum

Dictator
An amusingly shaped root vegetable

Diffident
Novelty toothpaste

Digression
Welsh fighting talk

Dilate
To live long

Dilatory
Conservative sex aid

Dildo
Pickled pastry

Diphthong
To wash an undergarment

Direct
Ruined by a Welshman

Disappear
To insult a Lord

Dd

Fig.25 Discount

Disconsolate
A particular embassy

Discount
Making clear which member of the nobility you
are talking about

Discover
A record sleeve

Diverging
An unsuccessful Welsh lothario

Dodo
A repeat of 'The Simpsons'

Dogma
Bitch

Fig.26 Dogma

Domineering
An earring shaped like a domino

Dossier
A French tramp

Doughnut
An eccentric millionaire

Dunderhead
An exclamation by a sculptor after he has finished
the top part of a bust

Ee

BRICK LANE E1

Fig.27 Enrage

Ee

Egocentric
The yolk

Eldorado
Didn't seem like a good idea in the first place

Elegy
An inflammatory reaction to poetry

Elemental
A Spanish village idiot

Emboss
To promote to the top

Enrage
A row about poultry
in the East End

Ersatz
A Somerset milliner

Fig.28 Elemental

Ee

Equip
An unasked-for joke off
the internet

Esplanade
Attempting an explanation
when drunk

Ethics
The place where girls with
white stilettos live

Eureka
B.O.

Evanescent
A Welshman who glows in the dark

Exclaim
Alimony

Fig.29 Eureka

Expense
Old money

Expensive
No longer thoughtful

Explain
Concorde

Extemporary
Permanent

Extort
Having left school

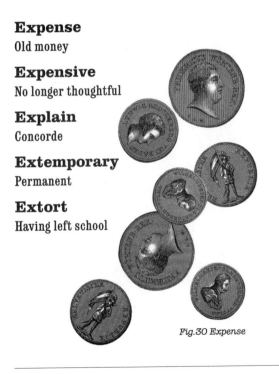

Fig.30 Expense

Ff

Fig.31 Flatulence

Ff

Feckless
a. A censored version of 'Father Ted';
b. An unsuccessful Irish lothario

Fecund
The one before 'fird'

Fiasco
An unsuccessful wall painting

Fibre-optics
The healthy alternative to eye candy

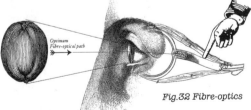

Fig.32 Fibre-optics

Finesse
A woman from Finland

Ff

Five-a-side
To kill a boy band

Flatulence
An emergency vehicle that picks you up after you have been run over by a steam roller

Flemish
Prone to spitting

Flippant
A glib insect

Follicle
A tiny little ruin
built on a small hill

Fondue
An affectionate sheep

Fig.33 Fondue

Forbearing
A group of pregnant
women

Forecast
Fishing before
anyone else

Foreskin
To compel relatives

Fig.34 Forebearing

Fornication
Communication between golfers

Frigate
A ship that nobody cares about

Frog-spawn
Blue movies for the French

Fuselage
Not many that big

Fig.35 Guacamole

Gg

Gargoyle
An olive-flavoured mouthwash

Gazette
A baby antelope

Geiger counter
Device for measuring the
skill of ventriloquists

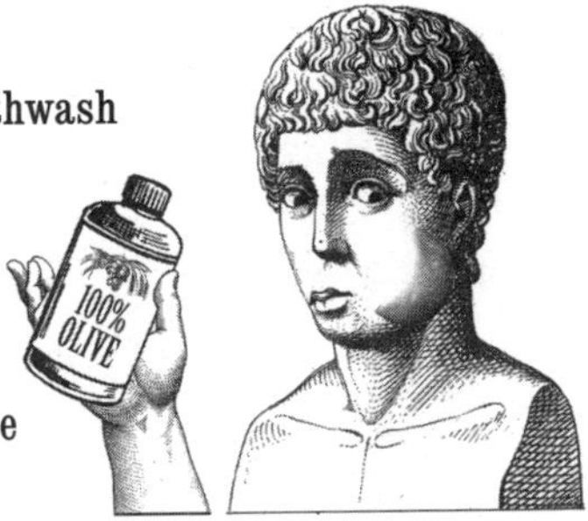

Fig.36 Gargoyle

Genealogy
An aversion to denim

Geranium
The cry of the Parachute Regiment's Flower Arranging
Display Team

Geriatric
Three goals scored by Germans

Gg

Gigolo
Jennifer Lopez running

Gonorrhoea
Behind with the rent

Graffiti
Newton's Law of Dyslexia

Granary
An old folk's home

Fig.37 Gripes

Gripes
What Australians make wine from

Guacamole
A Mexican visitor to Toad Hall

Gurgle
To steal a ventriloquist's dummy

Hh

Fig.38 Hobgoblin

Hh

Hacksaw
A tabloid report

Haddock
An enclosure for sea horses

Haemorrhage
A line of piles

Haphazard
Mind that hap!

Harlequin
One of a set of five motor-bikes

Harpist
Fairly drunk

Haywain
Essex greeting

Fig.39 Harpist

Heathrow
Brief description of what a baggage handler does

Hebrew
Jewish teabag

Hedgerow
Hedgehog eggs

Henceforward
Poultry advancing

Herpes
What my wife wins prizes for at the local flower show

Hiding
A bell you can't reach

Hindsight
Jennifer Lopez (see 'gigolo')

Fig.40 Hiding

Hh

Hirsute
Ladies' clothing

Hither
A snake with a hair lip

Hoarding
A prostitute's microwave

Hobgoblin
Eating stoves

Fig.41 Hirsute

Hobnob
A cooking accident

Hobnobbing
Casual sex with a goblin

Hogmanay
Someone who may be considered to have too large a collection of a particular Impressionist painter

Hirsute – Humbug

Homophobe
Somebody who doesn't like 'The Simpsons'

Hopscotch
One-legged Glaswegian

Horticulturalist
Brian Sewell

Hosepipe
A dance by sailors wearing socks

Hotpot
Stolen drugs

Hullabaloo
How to greet a bear

Humbug
A musical insect

Fig.42 Humbug

Hh

Humdinger – Hydraulics

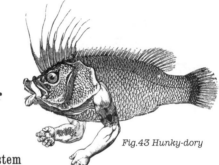

Fig.43 Hunky-dory

Humdinger
A fly swat

Humphrey
A good sound system

Humpty Dumpty
One who is humped and dumped

Hundred
A fear of Germans

Hunky-dory
A butch fish

Hydraulics
To conceal the things that you rest your oars in

I i

Fig.44 Idiomatic

Ii

Iconography
Filthy Byzantine pictures

Idiomatic
A Ugandan washing-machine

Impact
Goblin stand-up

Impart
Goblin painting

Impeccable
Bird proof

Implication
An ointment for little goblins

Inclement
Freudian slip

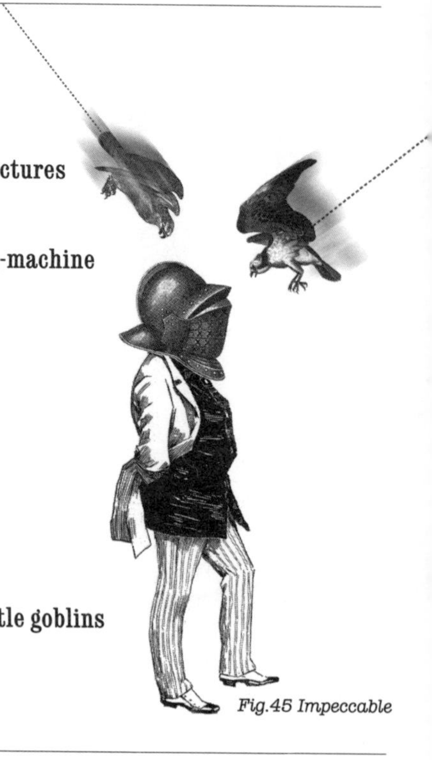

Fig.45 Impeccable

Income
Entrance

Increment
The opposite of excrement

Indelible
a. A bull in Delhi;

Fig.46 Inhabit

b. A person who cannot be persuaded to eat bagels

Indict
When the Queen is unsure about something

Inhabit
Dressed as a monk

Innuendo
An Italian suppository

Insolent
To fall off the Isle of Wight ferry

Ii

Integrate
Answer to the question 'where's t'coal?'

Intense
Camping

Intent
Determination to go camping

Intercontinental
A person who has wet
themselves all over the world

Investment
Thermal underwear for bankers

Ipod
Optical aid using peas

Ipswich
What you turn your hip on with

Fig.47 Ipswich

 j

Fig.48 Judicious

Jj

Jacobites
Michael Jackson's range of snacks

Jasmine
Kenny Ball's band

Jigsaw
Chaffing that affects the cast of 'Riverdance'

Jihad
The cry of the fundamentalist cowboy

Jocular
Funny eye

Jocularity
Laughter on horseback

Judicious
Hebrew crockery

Judo
Kosher plasticine

Fig.49 Kirby Grip

Kk

Ketchup
To draw level

Khaki
A device for starting an automobile

Killjoy
Gloomy East Anglian antiques dealer

Kilometre
Device to calculate extent of slaughter on talent shows
(cf: Pol Pot's record-breaking appearance on 'Opportunity Knocks')

Kinship
An unpopular boat

Kirby-grip
North Yorkshire handshake

Kitten
Hit by a kite

Knapweed
A damp sheet

L l

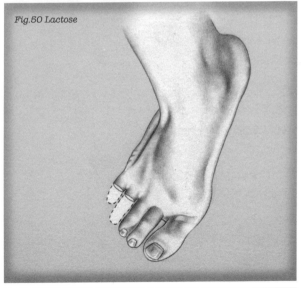

Fig.50 Lactose

LI

Lackadaisical
Short of one flower

Lactose
Frostbite

Laminated
Pregnant sheep

Lamination
New Zealand

Fig.51 Lamination

Lampoon
A device for whaling at night

Lassitude
To have been bitten by a collie

Legal
A sixteen-year-old bird of prey

Leprechaun
A variety of wheat whose ears fall off

Libel
An Australian price tag

Likeness
Highlands enthusiast

Limpet
A little limp

Lipsynch
A lady's intimate
wash basin

Livery
Rather like liver

Locomotion
A barely audible riot

Fig.52 Likeness

LI

Logarithm
Lumberjack's contraceptive

Logical
A very small Masonic meeting house

Loofah
An outdoor toilet

Loophole
A very long lavatory brush

Lupine
An air freshener

Lymph
To walk with a lisp

Lyricist
A complaint suffered by songwriters

Fig.53 Lymph

Fig.54 Melancholy

Mm

Macadam
A Scottish brothel-keeper

Macaroni
The inventor of the pasta wireless

Maisonette
A very small chief constable

Mangoes
He leaves

Manifold
Another word for origami

Manoeuvre
A vacuum cleaner even men can work

Margate
The mother of all scandals

Fig.55 Manifold

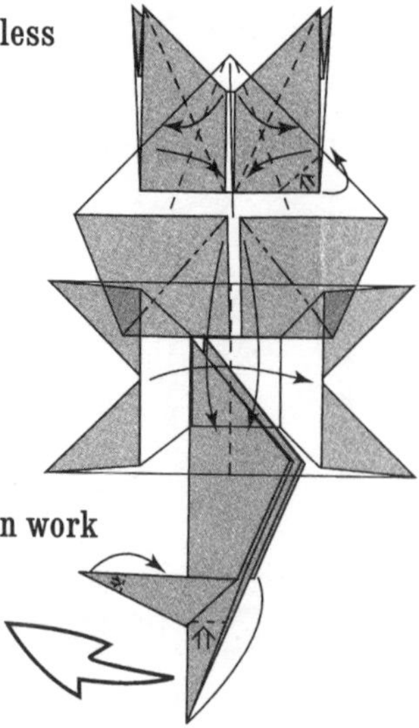

Marigold
Get rich quick

Marinade
A soft drink for weddings

Maritime
When the wedding starts

Marmite
An insect found on mothers

Martini
A very small
supermarket

Mascot
A Catholic nursery

Masseuse
A roomful of stutterers

Fig.56 Marmite

Mm

Mastiff
a. A row during a
church service;
b. Boys at a Britney
Spears concert

Meander
She and I

Melancholy
A funny-shaped dog

Mendacity
To rebuild a town

Merciful
Liverpool's flooded

Merseyside
The killing of Scousers

Fig.57 Meander

Microbe
A tiny little dressing gown

Microfiche
Sardines

Migraine
What a farmer calls his crops

Minimal
A small shopping centre

Minuscule
Toddlers' playgroup in Liverpool

Mischief
Head girl

Fig.58 Microfiche

Mistake
Winner of a butcher's
beauty contest

Mm

Mobster
An aggressive crustacean

Mogadon
My cat's a professor

Monochrome
A bath with only one tap

Moustache
Got to run

Morass
Request from the director of a strip show

Moreover
An overweight dog

Mosquito
A tiny place of
Muslim worship

Fig.59 Moreover

Mucus
A swearword used by cats

Multiple
To heat wine

Mushrooms
What Laurence Llewelyn-Bowen does

Mutant
A cross between a cat and an insect

Mutate
An art gallery for cats

Mystical
S&M for beginners

Myth
A female moth

Fig.60 Myth

Nn

Fig.61 Negligent

Nn

Navigator
Road-building crocodile

Negligent
Man who wears lingerie

Neighbourhood
The gangster next door

Fig.62 Nematode

Nematode
An avenging frog

Nonchalant
To arrive at Butlins
without prior booking

Notable
Full restaurant

Nurture
A Chas 'n' Dave song

O

Fig.63 Osmosis

Oo

Online
(Yorkshire) 'I've done t'weekly wash'

Orchid
The son of a Brummie

Orthodontist
One of those very devout dentists with the beards
and the hats

Osmosis
Early Australian prophet

Overrate
Nine

Oxymoron
Stupid cow

Oyster
Someone who likes to pepper his conversation with
Jewish expressions

Pp

Fig.64 Pandemonium

Pp

Palisade
What the Queen drinks

Pandemonium
A black and white musical instrument that won't
breed in captivity

Paradox
Two medical men

Paraffin
A flying fish

Paranoid
An angry person who
jumps out of aeroplanes

Fig.65 Paraffin

Parasites
Views from the Eiffel Tower

Parsimonious
Indian singer

Pp

Parsnip
Dad's vasectomy

Paterfamilias
A well-known comedy routine

Paucity
Liverpool

Pendulous
When you can put a pen under it and it stays there

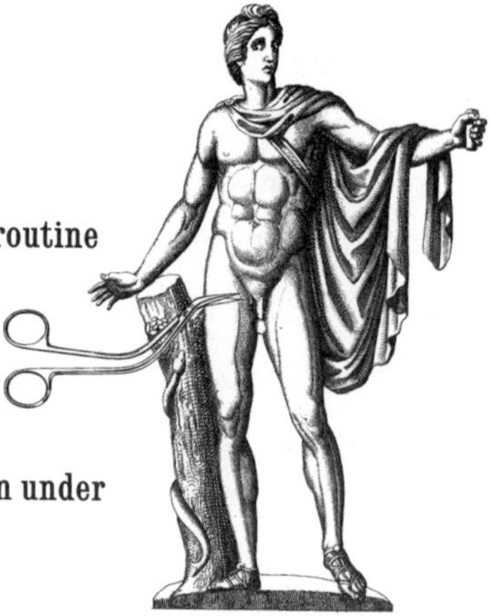

Pentecost
The price of posh ladies' knickers

Peripatetic
A disappointing chilli sauce

Persuade
To encourage somebody to buy Hush Puppies

Fig.66 Parsnip

Pharmacist
Agricultural swelling

Physique
A Perrier enema

Piano
A musical shipping line

Picador
Find your own way out

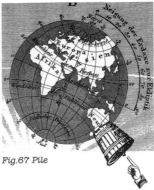

Fig.67 Pile

Piccaninny
The voting procedure for a new Tory leader

Pile
An Australian bucket

Pistachio
To draw a moustache on a poster when you're under the influence of drink

Pp

Piston
One who is taken
advantage of

Plaintiff
A row with a stewardess

Plantation
Bad police practice

Fig.68 Platitude

Platitude
The opposite of 'plongitude'

Plebiscite
Web page for common people

Plinth
Artist formerly known as having two speech defects

Plutocrat
Someone who votes for a Disney character

Pokemon
A Jamaican proctologist

Politician
A famous Italian painting of a parrot

Polygamist
A two-timing parrot

Polygon
A missing parrot

Polymath
A numerate parrot

Polyunsaturated
Dry parrot

Pomegranate
An Australian expression used to describe British stone

Pp

Fig.69 Pontificate

Pom-pom
An Australian word for English twins

Pontefract
To theorise about Yorkshire

Pontificate
A lecture on French bridges

Poppycock
A streaker on November 11th

Porcupine
A reluctant vegetarian

Porsche
Really, really posh

Portent
The Millennium Dome

Portly
Shaped like a harbour

Posterity
Inherited bottom size

Posthumous
The act of delivering Greek food by mail

Postulate
New name for Royal Mail

Pp

Poultry
A small amount of chickens

Preach
A soft fruit with a speech defect

Pre-Raphaelite
One who leaves before the raffle

Problematic
Dodgy loft conversion

Proletarian
Someone who only eats common people

Propaganda
A post for one-legged
male geese

Fig.70 Propaganda

Propane
People who are
into S & M

Fig.71 Property

Property
A decent cuppa

Prophylactic
Holder of the chair in milk

Psychiatric
Guessing right three times in a row

Psychopath
Crazy paving

Pulpit
Warren Beatty's bed

q

Fig. 72 Quaker

Qq

Quadrant – Quisling

Quadrant
Four people shouting

Quaint
Archaic form of 'quisn't'

Quaker
Posh duck

Fig.73 Quadrant

Quarterize
A cyclops when he's squinting

Quash
Quince cordial

Quietude
Ate silently

Quince
Not quite a coincidence

Quisling
Underdeveloped question and answer session

Rr

Fig. 74 Rugged

Rr

Raffia
Craft fair organised by crime syndicate

Rampart
Essential element
in sheep breeding

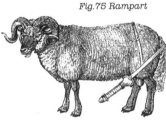

Fig.75 Rampart

Ramshackle
A male chastity belt

Rancour
A Japanese term of abuse

Ransack
The act of making someone redundant in a hurry

Ransom
A short amount of exercise

Rapscallion
A funky spring onion

Rr

Rebut
To have one's bottom lifted

Recordable
Sash windows you can fix

Rectitude
The angle at which a
thermometer should be inserted

Rectum
Indigestion

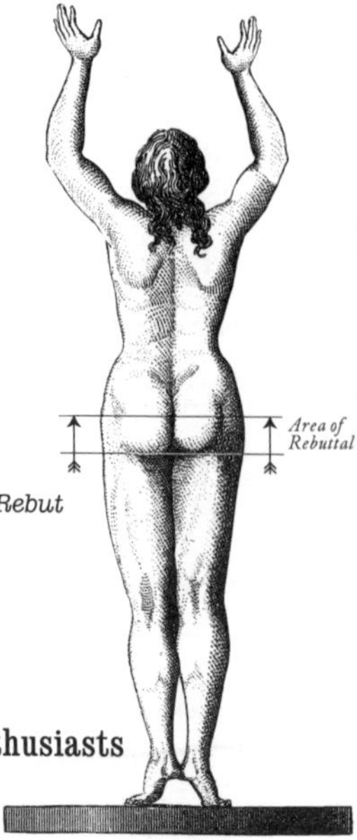

Fig. 76 Rebut

*Area of
Rebuttal*

Relief
What trees do in Spring

Renegade
Device for blowing up anagram enthusiasts

Renovate
To restore a French car

Retard
Very difficult in Yorkshire

Retread
Very red in Yorkshire

Revolt
To charge a battery

Rugged
Wearing a wig

Rugger
A wig-maker

Fig. 77 Rugger

S s

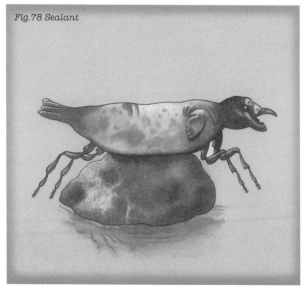

Fig.78 Sealant

Ss

Saab
Indian for 'nice car, master'

Samovar
Term describing how many and
whose planes are missing

Sanctity
Drooping bosom

Satellite
Burnt behind

Satire
Seated in a more
elevated position

Fig. 79 Satire

Level of Satire

Ss

Saxophone
Hotline to a salt
supplier

Scandal
Footwear you should be
ashamed of

Fig.80 Scandal

Scarf
To eat in Knightsbridge

Scintillate
To commit adultery till breakfast

Scooby Doo
A responsible dog owner

Scum
It has arrived

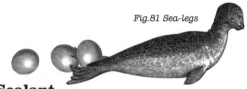

Fig.81 Sea-legs

Sealant
Amphibious insect

Sea-legs
The eggs of the seal

Secretariat
Headwear for typists

Secular
Junk mail in Liverpool

Sedate
Meant nine

Sentiment
The perfume he intended to buy

Ss

Sewage
Legal work

Shallot
No more onions

Shambles
Imitation brambles

Shambolical
Padded Y-fronts

Shampoo
Fake dog mess

Shamrock
Tribute band

Shellfish
A bit like a shelf

Fig.82 Sewage

Shingle
Sean Connery's definition of a bachelor

Shinto
Leg diagram

Shi-tzu
An unacceptable animal park

Shoehorn
A fetish

Signature
Baby swan droppings

Slippery
A bit like a slipper

Snickers
Spanties

Fig.83 Shinto

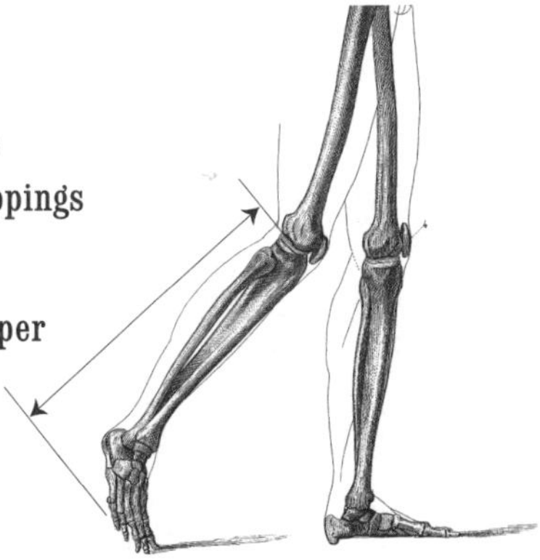

Ss

Sociopath
A serial killer who does wonders for your back pain

Somersault
Substance for de-icing the roads in July

Soupçon
Dinner's nearly ready

Spectacular
A short-sighted vampire

Fig.84 Spectacular

Spinach
Skin irritation caused by sitting too close to Alastair Campbell

Splint
To run very fast with a broken leg

Stalagmite
Prisoner-of-war camp for fleas

Star-struck
Nicole Kidman's lorry

Stockade
Meat-based fizzy drink

Stopcock
A condom

Strawberry
Grass hat

Stucco
Hitherto unknown
Marx brother

Stylist
Pig directory

Substitute
An underwater hooker

Fig.85 Stylist

Ss

Suffocation
A weekend in Lowestoft

Suffragette
a: Water spray for colonic cleansing;
b: A package holiday flight

Suggestive
A sexy biscuit

Supine
To take a tree to court

Surrogate
Stand-in Yorkshire Spa town

Sushi
Eddie Cantor's best known song: 'If you knew Sushi,
like I know Sushi'

Sycamore
Not as well as I used to be

t

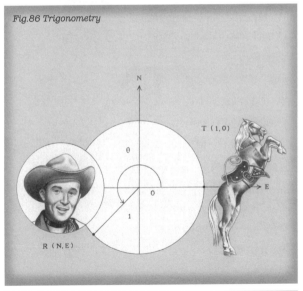

Fig.86 Trigonometry

Tt

Tadpole
A quarter Polish

Taffeta
a. Welsh goat's cheese;
b. A cannibal with a preference for Welsh people

Tannoy
To irritate loudly

Tantamount
To ride a French aunt

Tapas
To gently touch
someone's bottom

Tapestry
Ornamental plumbing

Fig.87 Tannoy

Tarmac
Scottish gratitude

Tatter
Poor quality milliner

Telepathy
When you can't be bothered to turn over the TV

Tendentious
False teeth

Tentacles
Prehensile genitalia

Tentative
Not sure about camping

Tepee
A small tent outside a wigwam

Testicle
An amusing exam question

Tt

Teutonic
What you order with 'two gin'

Thermidor
A Spanish lobster fighter

Thermos
The Greek God of picnics

Thespian
A woman who only sleeps
with actresses

Throng
A three-piece thong

Tickertape
Temporary watch strap

Tiddlywinks
A kip after a skin-full

Fig.88 Thermidor

Timbre
The cry of the French lumberjack

Titillate
Delayed puberty

Toadstool
Porn version of 'The Wind In The Willows'

Toga
A dyslexic goat

Tomahawk
A vegetable of prey

Tombola
A man who throws cats

Fig.89 Tomahawk

Toronto
Expression used by the Lone Ranger when drunkenly
addressing his colleague

Tt

Torpid
Incomplete torpedo

Torrid
Something horrible in Yorkshire

Trampette
A lady tramp

Trampoline
A cleansing fluid for tramps

Transistor
a. Brother who wears his mother's clothes;
b. Sex-change sibling

Trash
Yorkshire measles

Traumatise
Troubled neckware

Fig.90 Trifle

Trifle
A three-barrelled shot-gun

Trigonometry
A cowboy's method for
locating his horse

Trilby
A bee that rings

Tripod
A carrier for tripe

Truculent
Your kind loan of a Transit

Turpentine
A Geordie highwayman

Fig.91 Trilby

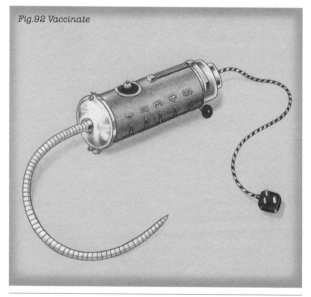

Fig.92 Vaccinate

Uu Vv

Umbrage
Angry clash between umbrella users

Undercarriage
Run over by a train

Urethra
Misspelt American soul singer

Usury
Japanese for 'usually'

Vaccinate
To administer drugs with a Hoover

Valpolicella
Mr Doonican's parrot is
in the string section

Vanilla
A large white ape

Fig.93 Vanilla

Vv

Vanish – Vocation

Vanish
Rather like a van

Varnish
To disappear in Mayfair

Vegetarian
Bad hunter

Veneer
Flemish painter of floorboards

Vespa
Evensong on a scooter

Vocation
Giving your voice a rest

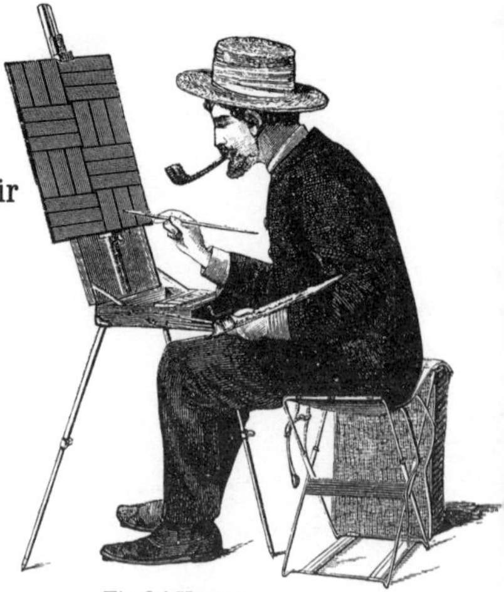

Fig.94 Veneer

Fig.95 Wallaby

Ww

Waif
Spouse (cf. 'you'll have met the waif?')

Walkie-talkie
A flightless parrot

Wallaby
Someone who aspires to
be a kangaroo

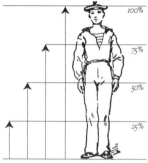

Fig.96 Wholesaler

Waxwork
Slogan for the 'Society for the
Restoration of Corporal Punishment'

Wench
A spanner belonging to Jonathan Ross

Wholesaler
Moby Dick's lunch

Wickerwork
Overseas TV journalism

Widdicombe
A brush to make your hair look like a wig

Willie-nillie
A cycling accident

Wink
Where Jonathan Ross
takes his children skating

Wisp
A really pathetic wasp

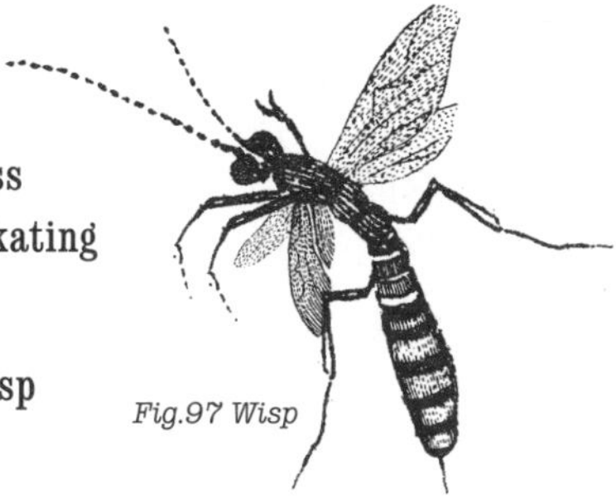

Fig.97 Wisp

Wisteria
Laughing till you wet yourself

Wonder
The period before Tudor

Wristwatch
All-night vigil in a very strict monastery

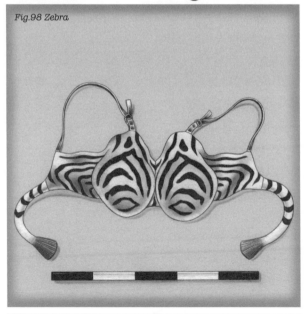

Fig.98 Zebra

Xx Yy Zz

Xenophobla – Zither

Xenophobia
Fear of Buddhists

Xerox
Jeffrey Archer's typewriter

Yankee
One who is yanked

Yarmouth
A flavoured wine from Norfolk

Yashmak
Shower-proof veil

Yonder
One who yonds

Zebra
The largest size of support garment

Zither
Yorkshire for 'look here'

Fig.99 Xenophobia

Foreign Words & Phrases

Fig.100 Trompe L'Oeil

Foreign words & phrases   A capella – Après ski

A cappella
The band hasn't turned up

Ad hoc
Liven up your rice pudding with a little German wine

Ad nauseam
Latest Benetton campaign

Annus horribilis
Do you mind if I don't sit down?

Après midi d'une faune
You've been on the telephone since lunch

Après nous le deluge
The lavatory's blocked

Après ski
a. Plaster of Paris;
b. I've finished the yoghurt

Foreign words & phrases

Au clair de la lune
Claire's a bit of a nutter

Avant garde
The next to last coach on the train

Avez-vous faim?
Would you like my sister?

Beaujolais Nouveau
Unsuitable for drinking

Belle époque
A cheap cut of pig meat

Bona fide
That's a genuine dog

Bureau de change
Superman's telephone box

Canneloni al forno
Al's fallen in the canal

Carpe diem
Fish of the day

C'est la guerre
a. Jumble sale;
b. Nautical outfits

Chacun à son goût
Oh, you like Pot Noodle do you?

Con allegro
A second-hand car salesman

Corps Anglais
French blokes lusting after English women

Cul de sac
My bag is in the refrigerator

Foreign words & phrases

Dieu et mon droit
The Bush family motto:
God And Me Are Right

Donna è mobile
A portable kebab stand

Donner und Blitzen
The after-effects of a kebab

Droit de seigneur
The gents is on the right

Et in arcadia ego
I had an omelette down the shopping precinct

Et tu Brute
Blimey you've splashed it all over and no mistake

Fiat lux
Car wash

Dieu et mon droit – Hors d'oeuvre

Film noir
The holiday photos haven't come out

Fin de siècle
Bicycle lover

Grand prix
Michael Winner

Hande hoch!
The white wine is at your elbow!

Hara-kiri
An opera singer educated at public school

Have a nice day!
Now bugger off!

Hors d'oeuvre
Ladies who hang around diesel pumps

Foreign words & phrases

Ich bin ein Berliner
I am a misprint for a bin liner

Ich dien
I am Jayne Torville's dancing partner

Ich liebe dich
I'm very fond of Richard

Infra dig
I'm an archeologist

In loco parentis
My dad's a train driver

La belle dame sans merci
The operator never says thank you

Magnum opus
a. Tom Selleck's cat;
b. An Irish cat

Mens sana in corpore sano
Corporal punishment is available in the men's sauna

Mi casa tu casa
My house has two lavatories

Moi aussi
I am an Australian

Non compos mentis
I don't think that's meant to be fertiliser

O sole mio
That's my fish

Petite chose
Your flies are open

Pinz nez
Not wearing underwear

Foreign words & phrases

Prima donna
Guy Ritchie's bachelor days

Requiescat in pacem
Our cat was totally ruined in the park

Sang froid
I'm dreaming of a white Christmas

Sic transit gloria mundi
Gloria was sick in the van but she'll be in on Monday

Spaghetti carbonara
My dinner's on fire

Steak tartare
The meat's off

Sub judice
The Israeli underground system

Tant pis, tant mieux
Auntie's been to the bathroom and she's feeling much better now

Trompe l'oeil
That one made my eyes water

Tutti frutti
Baked beans

Veni, vidi, vici
I came to see Vicky; unfortunately she was suffering from a social disease

Vin ordinaire
Ford transit

Abbreviations

Fig. 101 N.F.M.P.S

Abbreviations

A.A.A.A.
The Society For The Deaf

A.A.B.M.
The Association for the Abolition of Barry Manilow

C.I.E.C.
Campaign for the Impregnation of Edwina Curry

C.O.P.E.C.
Colin On Piano Empties Concert Halls

C.S.K.
Keep Spelling Correct

C.S.R.H.H.
The Conservative Sisterhood For The Re-election Of Herr Hitler

M.S.U.L.
Marks & Spencer's Underwear Leaks

Abbreviations

N.F.M.P.S.
National Front Medieval Poetry Society

R.F.C.M.C.
Radio Four Can Murder Comedy

U.S.W.D.
Unbearably Sexy Winter Drawers

FIN